What shall we call Wibbly's Puppy?

Mick Inkpen

Hodder
Children's
Books

A division of Hachette Children's Books

Wibbly Pig has
a new puppy.
'Aaaaah, isn't he lovely!
What shall we call him?'
'He's not very big,'
says Tiny Pig.
'We should
call him. . .

Tiny!

Just like me!'

'It would be much funnier if we called him **Big!**' says Big Pig.

'No, it wouldn't!' says Tiny Pig.

'Yes, it would!'

'No, it wouldn't!'

It is just as well that the Pig Twins have arrived.

I still
think
Tiny
is a
good
name.

'We should call him **Patch!**' say the Pig Twins, pointing to the patches on their heads.

The Twins agree that Patch is an excellent name.

But nobody else does.

Everyone thinks and
thinks and thinks and thinks.
But the more they think,
the more **nothing** happens
inside their heads.

'Let's find Pig Ears and ask him,' says Wibbly Pig. 'He's good at thinking.'

What's wrong with Tiny?

Pig Ears thinks
for a very long time.

He thinks for so long the puppy wanders off

and does a little poo.

Then
he falls
asleep.

At last Pig Ears speaks. . . .

'He's got nice sticky up ears,' says Pig Ears. 'Why not call him Ears?'

It is the worst suggestion yet.

Spotty Pig arrives. But before he can say anything, everyone says, 'We're not going to call him

Spot!

(Besides, it's been done before.)

So what are we going to call him?

‘Can't anyone think of a good name?’

Along comes
Scruffy Pig.
'I like your
new puppy!'
says Scruffy Pig.

We all stare at
Scruffy Pig.
We all stare at
the new puppy.
'Look at them!

Look!

They're **identical!**'

I don't know
what 'identical'
means!

'It means he's
exactly the same!'
says Scruffy Pig.
'Exactly the same
as me!

And my name is
Scruffy, so we
should call him
Scruffy, too!'

'Scruffy Two!'

says Wibbly Pig.
'That's what we'll call him!

It's even better than Tiny!

It's better than Tiny!
It's better than Big!
It's better than
Patch, or Ears,
or Spot.
It's perfect!'
says Wibbly Pig. . .

'Woof!'
says Scruffy Two.